Illustrated by Raymond Reyes

Shea –Shea Shea–na–ni–gans

Shea goes to the Doctor

Rev. date: 07/31/2013

To order additional copies of this book, contact:
Xlibris Corporation
1-888-795-4274
www.Xlibris.com
Orders@Xlibris.com

Shea–Shea Shea–na–ni–gans

Shea goes to the Doctor

by
Lana Schneider

Illustrated by Raymond Reyes

As humans, we all have to go see the Doctor every once in a while to make sure that we are healthy, or to help us get better if we are sick. Doctors give us medicine when we need it.

Shea had to go to her doctor to get a check-up. Animal doctors are called "Veterinarians". Veterinarians make sure that animals stay healthy, and get their medicine when they need it.

Shea and her owner entered the doctors office and were escorted into a special private room where there were lots of tools and gadgets, AND doggie treats. Her owner told her that she could have a treat when the doctor was done with her check-up.

The doctor walked into the office and proceeded to talk to her owner about any health concerns she might have about Shea. This information is very important to the veterinarian because he needs to know about Shea's health in order to help her.

Then the doctor needed to see how much Shea weighed so she had to get on a special doggie scale. The scale was wobbly and cold. This made Shea a little nervous, but she did it. She was being good so that she could get a treat afterwards.

Next, the doctor had to feel around Shea's body to look for any strange bumps that may be hiding in her body under her fur. He had to listen to her heartbeat, and take her temperature. He also had to look into her ears to see if they were clean.

He even shined a light in her eyes to make sure they were healthy too. Even though Shea wasn't in any danger, she still felt a little scared because she wasn't used to being handled in this way.

The doctor told Shea's owner that Shea had to get some medicine through a shot. Shea didn't like this idea. She was nervous that it would hurt too much and make her sad and cry. Shea sat very close to her owner hoping that the doctor wouldn't be able to find her to give her the shot, but hiding didn't work.

She was anxious and wanted to leave the room, but her owner grabbed her by her leash and held her close, kind of like a hug. Shea felt comforted by her owner doing this. Still scared and a little shaky, Shea got her shot. More than one actually. Neither one of them hurt and they were over very quickly.

When the shots were done, Shea got praises from the doctor and her owner. She liked this very much because that meant she was doing a good job and was going to get her treat soon.

Sure enough, the doctor opened the treat jar and gave Shea a delicious doggie treat. Crunch, crunch, crunch, it was so good. Shea politely asked for a second treat. Since she did so well, the doctor gave her another. Crunch, crunch, crunch, down her throat it went.

When the doctor visit was over, Shea and her owner went home. Shea was so proud of herself. She realized that there is no reason to be afraid of seeing a doctor.

She knew that her owner would keep her safe and that the doctor would be gentle with her. Shea always remembered to get a treat at the end of each visit, which was always the best part.

The End

This book is dedicated to my wonderful husband

Edwards Brothers Malloy
Thorofare, NJ USA
June 12, 2014